alanaolsen

there's no place like time

a retrospective

december 2018

alanaolsen

in collaboration with aila olsen

alanaolsen

I Am What You Have Forgotten

aila olsen | nov 2018

:::: *That's her father filming.* Her mother. An uncle. A family friend. I don't know. There's no record, of course. But look at that quiet assurance in my mother's eyes, that cool certainty. Her future seems unequivocally secure to her. She can be anything she wants, knows the end of her story at its beginning.

Except for one thing: she doesn't.

alanaolsen

:::: *She doesn't know* that two years after she died she would already have been almost forgotten. Yet to write that sentence suggests once she was relatively well-known. She wasn't, not outside a small handful of friends, family, fellow artists. She produced fewer than 20 videos over the course of her life. Some are missing.

Sorting through her belongings after her death, my brother discovered a slip of paper taped to the wall next to her desk, on it an unattributed quote:

The only hope for the survival of rock art is obscurity.

:::: *Another way of saying this:* This retrospective wonders what an aesthetics of obscurity looks like. What is the relationship between quality in art (whatever we might mean when we use that word) & quantity? What city in this conversation does my mother inhabit, & how? Is it possible to produce a space where her voice, mine, others interweave productively?

:::: *My father went missing* shortly after my mother died. I assume he's gone, too. Assume he killed himself after my mother succumbed, like so many others during the pandemic, to The Frost's growing sensation of coldness & amnesia.

My father simply vanished. A manuscript I choose to believe he wrote—a novel, perhaps; perhaps an autobiographical imagining of his own demise—showed up on my doorstep in Berlin. I conversed with him in its margins.

The slip of paper below the first taped to the wall next to my mother's desk reads:

Maybe life is simply a process of trading hopes for memories.

alanaolsen

We Don't Have to be Anywhere

:::: *Because this is one minute* & thirty seconds of family footage my brother found among my mother's belongings.

When these frames were shot, my mother didn't know she would marry an unsuccessful musician named Jeremy Ausfelder. Move to Brussels so he could attend medical school for a year before flunking out. Divorce him. Work as a car mechanic in Hackensack, New Jersey, not far from where she had grown up. She didn't know she would decide to enroll in a community college & launch her life over again.

Here she is learning you can run across your front yard with your eyes closed, playing a game with the neighborhood kids, for no reason at all.

Here she is learning we don't have to be anywhere.

:::: *Because* she became herself when she received a hand-me-down movie camera from her father (a sea captain away six months each year) on a family vacation to Niagra Falls. She was eight, ten. You can see her primary instinct is curiosity. Undoing beeline narration. Foregrounding shape, color, motion.

She thinks with her eyes: What can film do, & how, & why?

Her brother, like mine, is very nearly absent from her cosmos.

:::: *Because* early on she gains an insight that rhymes with Roland Barthes':

Every Photograph is
this Catastrophe

What My Mother Didn't
Know

alanaolsen

In front of the photograph of my mother as a child, I tell myself: She is going to die. I shudder ... over a catastrophe which has already occurred.

Whether or not the subject is already dead, every photograph is this catastrophe.

:::: *Because* there is no because— not in the way grammar would have us believe, so from here on out I leave it behind.

:::: *This retrospective* is comprised of videos, texts, objects, hypotheses, interventions. The composite doesn't seek to replicate, replace, or stand in for the past. It doesn't seek to function as immutable historical documentation.

It is rather meant to suggest a choreography, a way of moving through experience.

:::: *An archive* of unlearning.

alanaolsen

:::: *My mother* was born Alana Mc-Cord on 14 October 1955 in River Edge, New Jersey, just a few miles & 17 years away from earthwork artist Robert Smithson's birthplace.

:::: *The approach* this retrospective takes can be likened to a Wunderkammer, where distinct objects, lifted from their original situations, converse with one another, inviting the reader to remember, digress, discover, imagine.

:::: *I work as an* art critic in Berlin because, I tell myself, quite possibly wrongly, my mother made one of her most important films there.

:::: *In 1976 she* transfers to Fairleigh Dickinson University, in 1977 to Portland State, where she double majors

That Would Be
Somebody Else's Story

[[It Always Is]]

alanaolsen

The Problem with Tenses

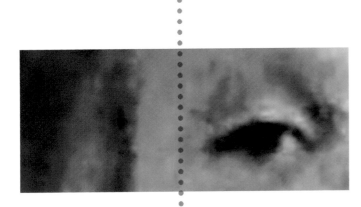

[   ]

in studio art & art history & meets my father, the man who will disperse, for want of a better word, 39 years later.

:::: *What I want* to emphasize here is this: I was never especially close to her.

    We had no special mother-daughter bond, no memorable moments. We weren't best friends. We were hardly even amiable acquaintances.

    That would be somebody else's story.

    [[It always is.]]

:::: *Collage is a form* of citation carried to its extreme.

:::: *The marvel that* there exists in our universe this observation by Jacques Derrida:

    Every sign, linguistic or non-linguistic, spoken or written (in the usual sense of this opposition), as a small or large unity, can be cited, put between quotation marks; thereby it can break with every given context, and engender infinitely new contexts in an absolutely nonsaturable fashion.

alanaolsen

:::: *Think of all* the photographs embedded inside every film.

:::: *If I'm being* honest with myself, there was a lot about my mother I didn't like. How she could shut me out with a single quick look. How it was always her show. How sometimes she made me feel like a footnote in her text.

I should add, in case there might be any room for misconstrual, she didn't particularly like me, either.

:::: *In the end,* there is always a certain problem with tenses.

:::: *For months* my mother wouldn't work on a film. She would clean out the garage instead. Respond to long-forgotten emails. Garden. Help my father down at his bookstore, The Used Appendix. Spend three weeks straight fighting City Hall so

alanaolsen

Salt Lake would fess up & pay for the gutter on our garage
its garbage truck's mechanical arm accidentally dented.

My brother & I would wake one morning to find
the door to her office shut. My father would take charge, or
maybe we'd simply be left to our own devices.

My mother would suddenly become footsteps thumping
through the nights.

:::: *You don't,* it turns out, have to like another person in order to love them.

:::: *Or Robert Smithson,* echoing Claude
Lévi-Strauss:

*"Entropology," not "anthropology," should be the word
for the discipline that devotes itself to the study of ... disintegration in its most highly evolved forms.*

:::: *You don't,* it turns out, have to understand another person in order to love them, either.

:::: *Love, I now* understand, is a different choreography altogether.

alanaolsen

:::: *And so my* mother meets my father, marries him, receives her B.A., & enrolls in the graduate program in studio art at the University of Washington—all in the same year Mark David Chapman steps out of the shadows, calls John Lennon's name in the carriageway of the Dakota, & acquires a combat stance.

:::: *All children* *have to be deceived if they are to grow up without trauma*, Kazuo Ishiguro reminds us.

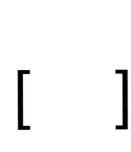

:::: *The manuscript* that I choose to believe my father wrote showed up in a plain mailing envelope on my doorstep without a return address. It was typed on an old manual. I conversed with him in its margins, underlining or bracketing words that felt important to me, thinking through them into my life, talking to him in ways we never did while he was here.

:::: *Everything will be* okay in the end, John Lennon once said. If it's not okay, it's not the end.

:::: *My brother Lance* edited the manuscript.

He titled it *Theories of Forgetting*, found a small press interested in it because it was related to my mother's small body of work, & the next year it was published, my marginalia and all.

Done, he mailed the original back to me.

On a holiday to Norway, I stayed in a cabin overlooking a fjord.

After a simple dinner I opened a bottle of good single malt, built a fire in the wood stove, and fed in the manuscript page by page.

:::: *Most people go* through life dreading they'll have a traumatic experience, Diane Arbus adds.

Freaks were born with their trauma. They've already passed their test in life.

They're aristocrats.

We are all aristocrats.

But maybe some more than others.

alanaolsen

We Are All Aristocrats

alanaolsen

1. man standing by phone booth waiting for call or maybe waiting for something else or maybe just passing time, nothing happens, 3 minutes.

2. woman chatting among group of friends in square abruptly turns, expressionless, & runs away, only she & I know it's performance piece

her notes about early film experiments in graduate school. [[none survives.]]

3. film the last three minutes of *Waiting for Godot* backwards, then play it forwards in continuous loop, the familiar returning as the unfamiliar

alanaolsen

[[Some More Than Others]]

alanaolsen

homeless man standing alone in park, arms scare-
crowed at his sides, pedestrians flowing around him.
imperceptible performance piece #2

4.

imperceptible performance #3: film corner of world
that would happen anyway. viewers entering art gallery, lovers kissing by park bench, etc.

5.

she worked on her M.F.A. in
studio art for 7 years:
1980 - 1987

three minutes, male actor on stage playing King Lear
on heath, only without moving his lips, dub with
young woman's sexy voice, loop

6.

alana olsen

Where the Smiling Ends
| april 1985

:::: *Hugh & Alana couldn't afford* a honeymoon for three years, but they always knew it would be Italy when the time came. A natural for an artist in training. Within days of arriving in the summer of 1983, my mother started hanging around the big tourist sites—the Trevi Fountain in Rome, the Piazza della Signoria in Florence—surreptitiously filming people having their photos taken.

Not, however, capturing the moment of the click. Rather the moment just after, when the expression fades back from public to private.

How the smile always ends in what looks like loss.

:::: *How every parting gives* a foretaste of death, Schopenhauer once noting.

:::: *A study in portraiture.* And, in this sense, an argument for continuity in aesthetics that leads us back into prehistory, the Fertile Crescent, the problematics of representation in the key of gods & kings.

Yet there are no gods or kings here, simply the expression of the problematics.

The subject—always the typical middle-class vacationer—is unaware of her or his double-subjectivity: an object for two cameras separated by a split-second's temporal dislocation.

The unconscious lowering of the head, as if intuitively to wipe out the instant of feigned happiness in a return to everydayness. As if briefly to inhabit an internal place the camera can't enter, & yet always does.

:::: *An anthropology of loneliness,* which is to say a slo-mo geometry of isolation following the expectant flash of community.

What's stunning for me is the ubiquity of this gesture.

That same pensive frailty wherever you focus.

alanaolsen

:::: *David Foster Wallace:* *Everybody is identical in their secret unspoken belief that way deep down they are different from everyone else.*

:::: *It's remarkable to watch* the subjects gather before those fountains, beside those sculptures, in those squares whose names, pasts, & significance they wouldn't be able to discuss, often know virtually nothing about. They show up because it's assumed they'll show up.

This, they believe, is what tourists do, where they go.

Their expressions confirm: *I am having the good time I am supposed to be having.*

:::: *The use of slo-mo* & black-&-white argues against this, against being on script, against the very idea of scripts, as does the use as soundtrack of Samuel Barber's gorgeous, mournful second movement from his *String Quartet, Op. 11* in B-flat minor.

Barber was only 26 when he wrote *Adagio for Strings*. Yet in it you can hear the alcoholism, depression, & withdrawal that would mark his last 15 years of life.

Nonetheless, by all accounts Barber was a happy child raised by an educated & comfortable family in West Chester, Pennsylvania.

Freud observes: *We find a place for what we lose.*

Each of us has his own rhythm for suffering, observes Barthes.

alana olsen

alanaolsen

alanaolsen

:::: *Even this early in her development*, my mother becomes fascinated by events that usually occur outside the temporal & spatial frame, the conventional center of vision. I experience her documentation as a rupture:

I thought I've been paying attention my whole life, yet I have never seen this simple, obvious, ever-present gesture until now.

You watch her look back to those imperceptible performances of her early graduate years in which the participants frequently don't know they're participating & that almost (but not quite) go unrecorded.

You watch her trying to unforget the world repeatedly.

alanaolsen

Night Driving
(for A. O.)

mike christensen | april 2017

Something shudders into my high beams
before my nerves have a chance
to yank the wheel, an image rising
of those people whose bodies aren't revealed
erect inside their turtled cars till spring thaw.
A cat or skunk skitters through my brights,
and almost simultaneously the soggy *whomp*,
the rill of thumps like a kid's rubber ball
jittering beneath my rig. And then nothing—
darkness in the rearview mirror,
harsh headlights eating up the road ahead,
this thought clustering behind my eyes:
some things you just don't stop for,
as I plunge on through the night.

alanaolsen

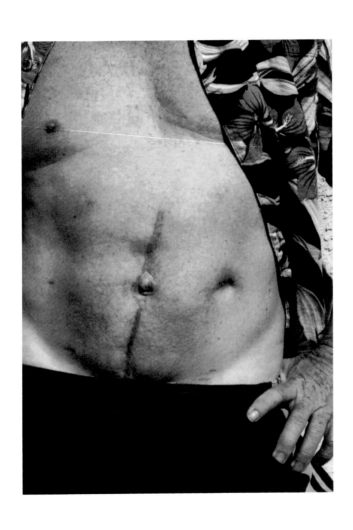

Scarred

r. m. berry | nov 1987

Alana Olsen approached me to appear in *Scarred* at a small conference in Seattle on intersemioticity—one of the first on the subject in the U.S., I
believe—late, I want to say, in 1985. I was an assistant professor at a local university
at the time. Olsen was still a graduate student. Her film *Where the Smiling Ends* had
screened a few months earlier at the DOXA Documentary Film Festival in British Co-
lumbia. I had happened across it in a group show called *In the End They All Will Die*
at the Pound Gallery on 10th Avenue, and I was impressed by its haunting, revelatory
quality. Olsen & I spoke in passing. She struck me as quiet, thoughtful, inquisitive,
careful with words. Her husband, Hugh, had wandered away to look at the rest of the
show & Alana seemed nervous & abandoned as we talked. She clearly didn't like the
attention or the crowds. She had the uncomfortable expression of a high-schooler who
had just showed up to a party at which she knew no one & couldn't find the host.

None of that matters, of course. What matters is *Scarred.* Olsen
apparently swallowed her shyness at that conference—an act of dedication, I imagine,
to her project—& simply walked up to participants & asked if they had any scars they'd
like to talk about. If one said yes, Olsen ushered her or him off to a corner—a hallway,

an empty classroom, a stairwell—raised her camera, & began shooting. I always assumed scars would be private affairs for people. Just the opposite turned out to be the case. It felt a little as if Olsen had opened a confessional booth with her invitation. As news about her interviews spread through the conference, a line of participants formed. I was surprised by their desire to testify about what in most cases was invisible to the rest of us.

Olsen filmed more than 40 statements before beginning to edit back to what we see in the final iteration.

She was a fastidious artist, laboring as slowly with her films as with her sentences. It took her two years to finish *Smiling*, two to finish *Scarred*. Yet each is only a few minutes long. That knowledge makes me admire them even more.

A shot, after all, is just a shot until we begin to sense the weeks of thought that went into it. Most of us unconsciously value a piece of art precisely in relation to the amount of work invested in its making.

Olsen & I stayed in touch loosely for a while after that. She used to kid about herself in the letters we exchanged, saying she was a pixel-by-pixel filmmaker who considered English her second language. I asked her once, *Scarred* having just premiered at the WorldFest-Houston International Film Festival, if she ever thought about hiring a P.R. person, growing her career strategically like so many contemporary artists do. She had just received her M.F.A. after seven years, Hugh his Ph.D. They had moved to Salt Lake City where Hugh was planning to open a bookstore. She never responded to

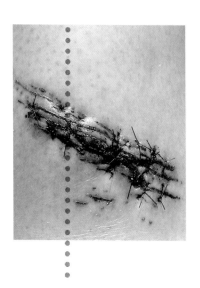 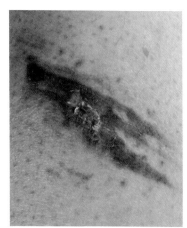 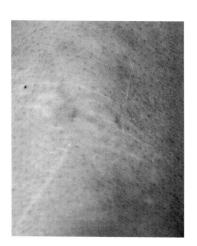

my question & I never heard from her again.

I think I understand her silence. It didn't prevent me from continuing to follow her work with great interest.

And then one day in April 2017 I received a note from her daughter announcing the memorial service. I was overwhelmed. I had no idea Olsen had even been ill. I still pictured her as that reticent graduate student I had met in Seattle.

I was teaching in Florida at the time—another job, another university—& couldn't easily get away during the semester.

And I never understood the logic of such final gatherings, so sent along both my condolences & my apologies for being unable to attend.

None of that matters, of course. What matters is that, at the end of the day, *Scarred* is all about how the world continuously writes upon us, reminds us where we've been, that that place is real.

After a certain amount of living, one's skin becomes a remarkable accomplishment. This is how gravity works, it says. This is what it looks like to have been alive. Children treat their scars like badges of honor, & for good reason. Lovers treat them like miraculous secrets. Old married couples treat them like familiar road signs.

I don't want to die without any scars, a character in Chuck Palahniuk's novel *Fight Club* declares at one point.

There is never any worry of that.

Every inscription that being leaves upon us—a split nail, a web of stretch marks, a zigzag of stitches—becomes a special hieroglyphics forming the map to what we have precariously named the self.

alanaolsen

That map calls attention to the paradoxical, flustering fact that the self is both always in flux & simultaneously constant. The participants in Olsen's film know this. Listen & look at them closely as they bear witness to these often relatively small, nearly un-noticeable scores upon their flesh, & what strikes one is exactly how important each of those scores is, what weight it carries.

We may think of all these emergencies of the flesh as scars, instances of a larger category, but every one is breathtakingly unlike every other—so long as we give our-selves permission to pay attention to the earth beneath the prose.

Still, every one tells some version of the same story: *I'm here. This is the proof against the feeling I sometimes have that I am nowhere. When this scar goes away, so will I.*

Or, to put it slightly differently, Merleau-Ponty: *The body is our general medium for having a world.*

The body is the part of our home that prompts us to remember we are never at home; that the body is our amusement park, our prison, and our grave.

[   ]

There's No Place Like Time

larry mccaffery | feb 1989

This is the existential moment: the long-distance call, the stutter step, the instant where nothing happens—where Nothing happens—again & again.

In a sense Alana Olsen's appropriation & repurposing of *Duck Amuck*, one of Chuck Jones' contributions to Warner Bros. Pictures' Merrie Melodies series in 1953 (in 1994 it was ranked by members of the animation field second of the 50 greatest cartoons of all time), is a joke. It's cartoon slapstick about our cartoon life, animated Keystone Cops. Listen closer & you can hear its laughter in the dark. Jones's piece is the Sisyphean scramble made flesh. The more one watches, the less easy it is to pass it off as mere distraction, some small flashy spectacle designed to make us turn our attention away from the heart of the matter.

Even upon first viewing, one senses the plot resonantly mythic in its simplicity: an unseen, godlike animator harasses Daffy Duck—Tex Avery's screwball everyman who starred in 133 shorts during the golden age of American animation—as locations, outfits, sounds, settings, & shapes continuously & contingently metamorphose in an elastic universe. At the end the sadistic animator reveals himself to be none other than Daffy's professional rival Bugs Bunny, offspring of such tricksters as Coyote & Loki.

Like so many of director Chuck Jones's pieces, behind the humor lies a horror, below the jokes an expression of all those things we are frightened to express. Olsen foregrounds this awareness by focusing on the few seconds in Jones' animation when the protagonist literally struggles against The End ... & loses; struggles against the way time happens at us. The temporal manifests as the spatial. Time turns material, &—again literally—there's no place like it. The visual argument of the work is that, although we may live with no other hope than becoming someone else's memory, something very different will always prove to be our fate. If Camus is one of the animation's

alanaolsen

real antecedents, Kafka is the other. With each frame, we hear his central understanding announced: *The meaning of life is that it stops.*

An interviewer once asked Donald Barthelme what advice he would offer young writers. One might expect the answer to have involved innovative form, perhaps a certain hardwired iconoclasm. Instead, Barthelme responded: *Write about what you're afraid of.* Writing about what she is afraid of (from the scripts imposed upon us to various sorts of dying) was always Olsen's intention. What changes from her juvenalia & graduate work to *There's No Place Like Time* is the key in which those fears are written. That key modulates over the course of her undertaking. The core obsessions don't.

Another way of thinking about *There's No Place Like Time*: the last decade of the 20th century witnessed the rise & proliferation of the Avant-Pop. A term appropriated by surfictionist Ronald Sukenick & me from a Lester Bowie jazz album by the same name, the Avant-Pop is a multi-media mode of expression that splices the avant-garde's fascination with innovation, experimentation, & radicalization with a deep pop sensibility. The result: an extreme fusion & confusion of the traditional distinctions between "high" culture & "low," an attempt to deploy the weapons of commodification against themselves.

In retrospect, one can trace the Avant-Pop's lineage back at least as far as Thomas Pynchon's & Andy Warhol's early efforts. Taking many forms, it surfaces in everything from William Gibson's cyberpunk novel *Neuromancer* (1984), which merges unusual techniques (surreal images, info-dense sentences, & the introduction of new vocabularies) with conventional science fiction conceits, to David Blair's cult film *WAX, or: The Discovery of Television Among the Bees* (1991), a disruptive serio-comic narrative about cross-sexual reincarnation & the Gulf War told by Mesopotamian bees (which turn out to be the souls of the dead). Think William Burroughs. Kathy Acker. David Bowie. David Foster Wallace.

Common to such creations is an often MTV-ized aesthetic that embraces speed, shock, high-tech, irony, data-thick consciousness, & (always ambivalently) the vast media-scape itself—a spectacular tele-geography on which Avant-Pop artists teethed. It is no surprise that

Every Photograph is this Catastrophe

What My Mother Didn't Know

The Meaning of Life is that It Stops

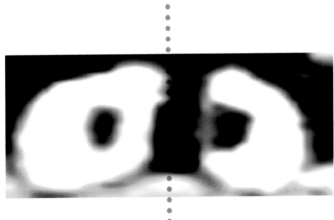

generation comprises the first to have been raised on myriad modes of popular culture. While Alana Olsen's larger project only brushed against the Avant-Pop's interests, & while her work remained unknown to most of her contemporaries, *There's No Place Like Time* has had a lasting effect on several experimental filmmakers who began their work in the late Eighties & early Nineties, especially Austrian Martin Arnold & Brit Douglas Gordon, both of whom are known for their obsessive reworkings of found pop footage.

Arnold builds his videos out of short intensely cut & manipulated sequences appropriated from iconic "low" cultural productions. Characters flicker & flutter-jerk as their movements, voices, & soundtrack repeat, reverse, slow, speed up. One analogy is the literary enterprise of erasure: Arnold seeks to unearth the filmic narrative beneath the filmic narrative. *Passage à l'acte* (1993), by way of illustration, uses several seconds from Robert Mulligan's film version (another sort of appropriation & manipulation) of Harper Lee's *To Kill a Mockingbird* in order to generate an uncanny story of aggres-

[   ]

alanaolsen

sion & tension within a traditional American family. Gordon, on the other hand, slows down found footage to a painful extent, recasting, for instance, Hitchcock's famous shower scene from *Psycho*, which in the original lasts 45 seconds, by showing two frames per second rather than the usual 24. The outcome is a crushingly unhurried film, meant to be projected on a translucent screen in an installation space, that lasts 24 hours & that, realistically, no one except Gordon has actually ever watched from start to finish.

Neither Arnold nor Gordon would have become the remarkable filmmakers they did, in terms both of visual and aural technique, without exposure to the early work of the relatively unrecognized Alana Olsen. She invited them to understand pop culture is the dream imagery we currently live, the imagery artists can use & abuse, a landscape they can tap into & short circuit to enlightening ends. Through Olsen's work, the unknown has leaked into the known. The margins of the marginal have moved to the margins' center, revealing the feminine always-already extant in the masculine. Viewers sense Olsen's presence in contemporary experimental film, that is, exactly by the presence of her apparent absence.

couple in dept. store trying to kiss, but something's
wrong, gestures awkward, slowly dawns on viewer
there's a pane of glass between them

7.

place camera on tripod in pioneer square, retreat,
let pedestrians interact, unaware they're part of
another imperceptible performance piece

8.

[[none of that matters, of
course.]]

shoot three frames each morning of bluejay decom-
posing on balcony, sans soundtrack, 365 days, play
backwards, watch it reassemble

9.

alanaolsen

Becoming Landscape
(for A. O.)

lance olsen | april 2017

The snake presents itself
        as a sluggish gray-green striped
squiggle in buffalo grass.

Ever since being a kid
        I've had to try
        a reptile's dignity
        with a stick.
I can't argue
        with that part of me.
So I locate a branch,
        nudge it beneath
        the snake's belly. Lift.

And the lower third of its flesh

just slips away,
boiled skin from chicken,
revealing moist red muscle,
lilac entrails, specks of bone.

Astonished, I let the thing
down again
gently as hope,
embarrassed at having interrupted
this dying.

It opens and closes its pink mouth
rhythmically in the yellow daylight.
Shadows skitter inside its skull like mice
while spruce, huckleberry,
columbine, time
corkscrew in,
close it off,
help it gradually tighten
into one more object
fixed in this landscape.

[   ]

alanaolsen

alanaolsen

Trace

christina milletti | july 1992

1

Narrative is never merely a form of escapism. One can never stand outside the political in a text. Just the other way around: narrative is invariably immersed in the political, especially during those moments it seems to be least so.

2

Entertainment isn't political. That's specifically what makes it so political. It invites us to forget, drift, pass time, lose ourselves in the familiar, which is to say in the agreeable.

3

Irigaray: the issue for the innovative is not so much to change the system as to resist its customary operation by *jamming the theoretical machinery itself ... suspending its pretension to the production of a truth & of a meaning that are excessively univocal.*

4

The issue for Alana Olsen in *Trace*—premiered at the Chicago International Film Festival in 1992; screened as part of the group show *The UnFair* at Vox Populi in Seattle a year later; screened at another (this one made up entirely of women artists), *Short Breaths*, at Galleri 8 in Portland the year after that—is to inject noise into the filmic system by following performance artist Tehching Hsieh through the streets of Lower Manhattan during the last few months of his *13 Year Plan*, the non-performance performance for which he made art, yet didn't exhibit it publicly.

5

Olsen transforms Hsieh's non-performance performance into her own by incorporating Hsieh himself into a performance he isn't aware he is a part of.

6

She further reverses & complicates the clichéd dynamics of the male gaze by becoming the female voyeur, Hsieh the subject made object. She then complicates the complication by adopting the role of visual colonizer, Hsieh the Asian unwittingly colonized, thereby pointing to the fact that we are all complicit in the construction & enactment of unequal & multivalent networks of power. No one, *Trace* argues, is ever innocent.

People Don't
Take Trips

Trips Take People

7

This includes Hsieh's handlers, who helped Olsen engineer the setup by agreeing to inform her where Hsieh would be and when.

Olsen donned the baggy costume of the quintessential American tourist & stood across streets in doorways with her camera, filming, usually out of Hsieh's direct line of sight.

The famous artist defined by his role's ability to see what others can't failed to see himself being seen.

8

Hsieh blindly belied his *13 Year Plan*, then, by becoming his own performance, his own piece of art publicly exhibited, which to say none of us can help ourselves.

alanaolsen

9

Further perplexing the visual grammar of *Trace*: no shot lasts longer than 20 frames—an idea that apparently lingered in Lars von Trier's imagination long after seeing Olsen's piece, possibly when screened alongside her *Arsonist's Guide to the Empire & Bare* at the Visionary Art Museum in Baltimore in 2000 when von Trier visited briefly to speak at Johns Hopkins University. This was the time, he has pointed out in more than one interview, he was thinking about his first set of constraints for Jørgen Leth in *Five Obstructions* (2003). There, of course, von Trier challenged his mentor in an aesthetic Oedipal struggle to remake Leth's seminal avant-garde short, *The Perfect Human* (1967), by re-shooting the film in Cuba, with no set & no shot lasting longer than 12 frames.

10

Only 1:40 of Olsen's original 22-minute production survives. When the sole extant reel was unearthed by her daughter in a box of papers, CDs, & other footage in Olsen's office shortly after Olsen's death, an attempt was made to transfer it to a digital medium. Mold, however, had damaged most of its surface. This misfortune can be read as the reverse of itself, naturally: as the physical manifestation of Olsen's larger preoccupation with entropological processes, perhaps even as her final imperceptible performance—one that looks forward to her last film, *Theories of Forgetting*, her experimental documentary about Robert Smithson's famous earthwork located on the north shore of The Great Salt Lake, *Spiral Jetty.*

11

Trace's soundtrack is built from a looped monologue often recited too quickly & too softly to be understood. It performs an aural entropology that suggests either a consciousness in decline or a radically associative, hypnagogic one. Phrases throughout echo/appropriate ideas/passages from Smithson's own essays, indicating Olsen was already richly absorbed in his work only a few years after settling into Salt Lake City.

12

The trace, Derrida writes, *is not a presence but is rather the simulacrum of a presence that dislocates, displaces, and refers beyond itself. The trace has, properly speaking, no place, for effacement belongs to the very structure of the trace.* For Derrida each sign unfailingly contains a trace of what it doesn't mean, can't mean—& yet does.

13

For Olsen being alive unfailingly signifies embodying a past that never took place, existing in a way that discloses how we are & can be always only [[there.]].

alanaolsen

Trace
(Soundtrack Transcription)

christina milletti | jan 2018

... primordial sea ... Ballardian wasteland ... reservoir of blood ... day to day ... hour to hour ... second to second ... Impressionist perfection ... depending on the texture of the light ... how it veils ... what it stresses ... water's tincture ... quality of clouds ... consistency of atmosphere ... person you were when you observed it then ... when you observed it then ... people don't take trips ... trips take people ... one is liable to see things in maps that aren't there ... how every video you make ... that anyone will make ... will have its final viewer ... how in the end there will be no one left to matter to ... when I was a kid I used to love to watch the hurricanes come & blow the trees down ... rip up the sidewalks ... when I walked the bridge ... it was as if I were walking on an enormous photograph made of wood & steel ... the river beneath an enormous film that showed nothing but continuous blank ... all this seeing ... all this relentless taking in ... primordial sea ... Ballardian wasteland ...

alana olsen

[[Rip Up the Sidewalks]]

An Arsonist's Guide to the Empire

davis schneiderman | oct 1994

Empire State, *Andy Warhol's 8-hour* silent movie of the New York landmark shot from a fixed perspective from 8:06 p.m. on July 25th to 2:42 a.m. on July 26th, 1964, at the offices of the Rockefeller Foundation, commences with a white screen, a blank, an opportunity. As the sun sets, a vaporous image of the icon emerges. Its exterior floodlights ignite, flicker for the next six & a half hours &, in the penultimate reel, dim. The rest of what we see takes place in nearly complete darkness. During three of the reel changes, the shoot recommenced before the lights in the filming room were switched off, making the ghost faces of director Warhol & cinematographer Jonas Mekas momentarily conspicuous in the window's reflection.

Filmed at 24 frames per second, *Empire* screens at 16. So, although only six hours & 40 minutes were shot, the movie becomes eight hours & five minutes long when screened.

Empire's *importance lies not so much* in its execution as in the audacity of Warhol's attempt to translate artmaking into philosophical act. He demands that viewers perform practiced attention in order to do nothing more than watch time pass & concentrate on that passing. As if to drive home the point, Warhol never allowed abridged screenings of his film.

Its very unwatchability is its reason for being.

In An Arsonist's Guide to the Empire, of which no copies exist

(mold, the filmmaker's daughter discovered, had destroyed the sole one), Alana Olsen pays homage to, collaborates with, & discomposes Warhol's experiment.

Olsen shoots the Empire State from precisely the same viewpoint Warhol did, yet rather than producing eight hours & five minutes of footage by slowing down a six-hour-&-40-minute shoot, she creates an eight-minute-&-five-second video by speeding up six-years-&-four-months of filming. By taking only a few frames every day, she, like Warhol, invites the audience to dwell on how time occurs, yet in a completely different way and for completely different ends.

She presents the viewer, not only with a meditation on the velocity of the contemporary, but also with an investigation into the unaccounted for.

While Olsen's attempt initially may strike one as imminently watch-

able, it soon becomes obvious that unwatchability is its objective. What you don't see, over and over again, is how the Empire State was completed ahead of schedule, taking 3400 workers on site at a time just over a single year to raise. You don't see how it cost $24,718,000 &, thanks to the Depression, came in under budget. You don't see

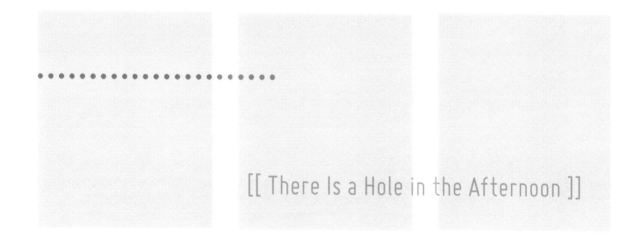

[[There Is a Hole in the Afternoon]]

the five people who died on the job or how the building's distinctive Art Deco spire was originally designed to act as mooring mast for dirigibles, a vision plucked from some H. G. Wells fever dream, but which proved to be impractical & dangerous due to the powerful updrafts caused by the size of the structure itself.

The complete history of New York over the course of the last
six years and four months thrums through *An Arsonist's Guide* by that history's very un-thereness. The viewer sees everything he or she can't see, from the late August 1991 Crown Heights riot pitting blacks again Orthodox Jews in the aftermath of an

alanaolsen

Time Is Always on Fire

unintentional car crash that left one Guyanese child dead & another severely injured, to the first World Trade Center bombing on February 26th, 1993. The viewer also sees what was never there in the first place: Fay Wray in King Kong's palm in 1933, Henry Fonda ordering bomber pilot Dan O'Herlihy to use the Empire State as ground zero in 1964, Tom Hanks and Meg Ryan wheeling up and down the edifice the same year a truck bomb packed with 1,336 pounds of urea nitrate–hydrogen gas was detonated beneath the North Tower four-&-a-half miles away.

All art, Olsen thereby contends, is a conversation across time & space, while all history is misremembered story. And all trauma will eventually become a strange form of nostalgia for that which never existed in the first place.

    For Olsen, time is always on fire.

The 1994 screening of *An Arsonist's Guide to the Empire* as part of *Short Breaths*, a women's group show at Galleri 8 in Portland, Oregon, marked the beginning of a five-year creative hiatus for Olsen. Her own history remodeled into a period of un-thereness.

alanaolsen

Little documentation survives concerning this chapter in her life, but through a series of interviews with her small circle of close friends it becomes clear Olsen grew invisible comfortably & on purpose. It was as if one day she simply flipped off her already-minimal public presence like those exterior floodlights on the Empire State each morning & withdrew, needing both to let her own artwork grow behind her back & to fully embrace the quiet suburban rhythms she & her husband Hugh had established for themselves in the high desert of Salt Lake.

One year later she gave birth to her son, Lance, who would become an author & editor. Two years after that her daughter, Aila, was born. Aila would move to Berlin in her early twenties to take up work as a conceptual artist while supporting herself through her work as art critic in the thriving avant-garde community that after World War Two in many ways returned that city to its essence as a global center of radical aesthetic & existential freedom, the likes of which it last enjoyed in the late 19th & early 20th centuries.

One may be distantly reminded of John Lennon's withdrawal from public life in 1975 to become a househusband.

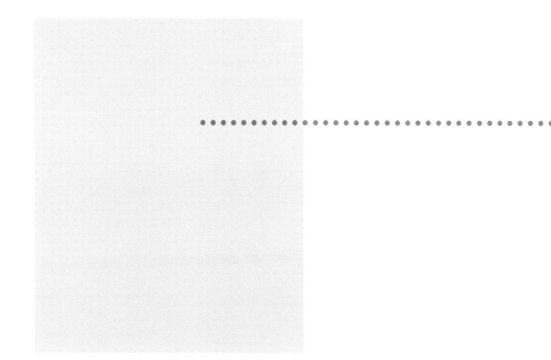

[[.]]

alanaolsen

For five years, he devoted himself exclusively to raising Sean, his son with Yoko Ono. Lennon spoke fondly of the sheer ordinariness of ahistorical life during that time. Unlike Lennon & Ono, however, Olsen seems to have been deeply unconcerned with anything that made her art feel to her like a business, & even less so with the emotional baggage accompanying a high profile in the art world.

Moreover, her increasingly fraught relationship with her children—& even with the very idea of having had children—has been well documented.

Over the course of her self-imposed pause from the public realm, Olsen apparently didn't remain completely dormant as a filmmaker. Several comments made by that close circle of friends point to a project she repeatedly tried & failed to begin between 1996 & 1999. Not even a title persists, let alone notes or footage. Yet, whatever shape that endeavor might have taken, Olsen in the end not only abandoned it, but also appears to have attempted eliminating all references to it. Neither her son nor daughter, needless to say, remember anything associated with its production. Her husband's disappearance & presumed suicide keep that blank blank. And, given her private nature, she only mentioned the project to her friends in passing, & in vague, even evasive terms.

⠿⠿⠿⠿⠿ ⠿⠿⠿⠿⠿⠿ ⠿⠿⠿⠿⠿⠿
⠿⠿⠿⠿⠿ ⠿⠿⠿ ⠿ ⠿⠿⠿ ⠿⠿⠿⠿⠿ ⠿⠿⠿ **10.**
⠿⠿ ⠿

⠿⠿⠿⠿ ⠿⠿⠿⠿⠿ ⠿⠿ ⠿⠿ ⠿⠿⠿⠿ ⠿⠿ ⠿⠿
⠿⠿⠿⠿ ⠿⠿⠿⠿⠿⠿⠿ ⠿⠿⠿⠿⠿⠿⠿⠿ **11.**
⠿⠿⠿⠿

[[none of that matters, of course.]]

From what those friends say, it is possible Olsen pursued what would have become her first & only feature-length film. One can imagine it would have dealt with her conflicted feelings about motherhood, about taking on that socially mandated role before having fully internalized its implications, & about doing so as a female in a culture that endorses—& often celebrates—a male artist's right to indulge in his art to the exclusion of family while tacitly expecting the female artist to conceptualize her creative work as simply one more facet in a primarily domestic matrix.

Whatever the case may be, that film (that ultimately isn't a film) forms yet one more blackout in a city full of them that makes up Alana Olsen's oeuvre & biography.

alanaolsen

alanaolsen

Bare

uljana weber | mar 2000

The idea crossed Alana Olsen's mind late in 1999 to video the young (at the time only 25) German performance phenomenon K. as he staged his latest piece: approaching strangers in their twenties on the streets of San Francisco, L.A., New York, & Berlin & offering to purchase everything on them on the spot—jeans, shirts, coats, watches, wallets, rings, chains, knapsacks, keys, sex toys, cell phones, chocolate bars, you name it.

Olsen evinced interest in the act itself, naturally, in her now-signature move of second-ordering & disarticulating the relatively easy assumptions associated with performance art & the relationship between performer & audience.

But she was interested in other issues as well. In an echo of the sociological impulse exhibited as early as *Where the Smiling Ends*, for instance—how the participants' expressions altered as they took in K.'s proposal on a busy corner, at a bus stop, in a crowded deli. How sometimes their faces went blank, the subjects simply turning & walking away as if approached for change by a homeless man. How sometimes their faces broke into conspiratorial grins as the subjects let themselves be led by K. into nearby department stores, coffee shops, clothing boutiques to do the deed. How K.'s visage (hair impossibly blond, face impossibly acne-wounded) never showed emotion as he waited patiently for them near the changing areas or restrooms while they stripped out of who they were & shrugged into the generic replacement clothes with which K. had provided them.

None of that, according to K., constituted the real performance. This came next, when K. returned to his makeshift studio at the end of the day &, his own video camera running, coated his subjects' possessions in thick gold paint almost to the point of unrecognizability, then arranged those objects with the care & precision of a model builder on a series of black plinths. Arrayed thus, the displays came to evoke, not simply an aesthetic moment, but also everything from taxonomical research to funereal rites, museum exhibits, pyramid treasures, & acts of cultural anthropology.

K. undergoes a metamorphosis similar to that through which he puts his subjects: he strips out of his role as artist & shrugs on that of scientist, shaman, curator, theorist, priest. Atop these is layered another: offspring of his chosen namesake, Kafka's Josef K. Like Kafka's character, K. bears no last name. Moreover, he has made it impossible to track one down in the records. His adopted accent has made it next to useless to place him with anything like certainty in Germany, Austria, or Switzerland. Some critics maintain he isn't from a German-speaking country at all.

alanaolsen

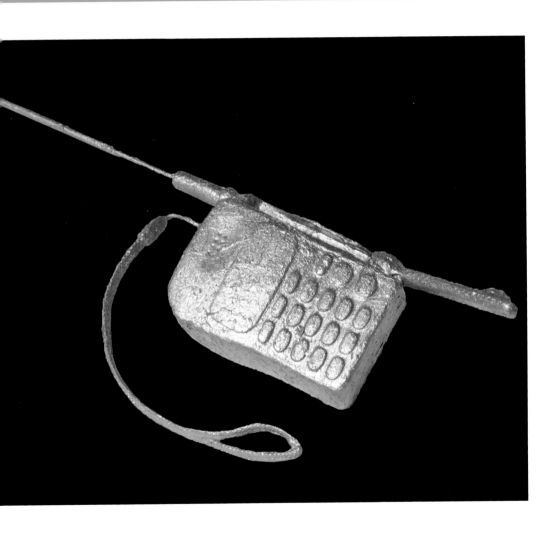

Be that as it may, Kafka's character informs K.'s persona: the essence of the humdrum human—sometimes arrogant, sometimes wracked with insecurity, always estranged—caught up in & used by impenetrable systems infinitely larger than he.

A less-well-known (if no less important) allusion residing in K.'s assumed name is to the relatively obscure Scottish post-punk band Josef K. (active between 1979 & 1982), whose songwriter, Paula Haig, was inspired by Kafka. Haig & Olsen met by chance at the LA International Shorts Festival where *Bare* screened in 2000. They maintained a sporadic email correspondence until Olsen's death.

Like Haig, K. affected an anti-rock stance, eschewing drink & drugs (which, Haig said, she found patronizing), working strict business hours, & actively embracing the idea of being manipulated by the art market in order to achieve success, even while acknowledging the absurdity of such hollow recognition. This in turn gained K. a higher profile as an outside-insider in the tradition of such wildly profitable (if carefully constructed) heretics as John Lydon & Banksy—one reason, perhaps, Olsen chose to cartoonize *Bare* as Richard Linklater would his *Waking Life* a year later.

The joke, then, is that everyone is in on the joke, yet can't help laughing anyway.

alanaolsen

Perhaps what drew Olsen most to this project was her critique of the suburban life she had been living, the one that had taken her away from her art for nearly five years. In the performance K. intended—as well as in those he didn't—Olsen underscores that we buy ourselves off the shelves of fashion boutiques & clothing franchises. We are literally what we own, what we carry on our backs & in our pockets & in our purses. Yet she also acknowledges that, even as we find ourselves moving through the day in that flustered, compromised position, we find ourselves inhabiting that position's opposite: unclothed, we pale into semi-absences, but our bareness implies that we're so much more than what stuff has made us.

Our possessions return us to the commerce that produces us rather than to the men & women we might be. Yet our bodies persist as powerful contrary traces. Still, even as we watch Olsen's video we can't help thinking that even those bodies are increasingly bought off various shelves lined with hair dyes, botulinum toxin, chemical peels, cosmetic fillers, & surgery.

Bare *screened four months* at the American Visionary Art Museum in Baltimore in early 2000 to positive reviews, & later that year in the LA International Shorts Festival; in the Rocky Mountain Women's Film Festival in Colorado Springs, &, finally, at the Banff Arts Centre in Canada, where Olsen spent a short residency. With *Bare* she once again locates her voice, & it is confident, fully in charge of its own vision & processes, indifferent to everything save where her inclinations might lead next.

alanaolsen

Everyone is in on the Joke

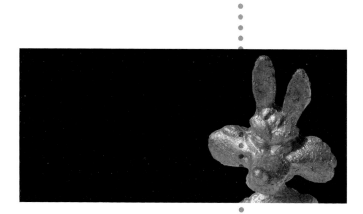

alanaolsen

Heaven Bent
(for A. O.)

paula haig | april 2017

One fine day when I've gone away
There'll be a voicemail on your phone
Telling you just what to say
When heaven calls to ask you home

When the invitation finally comes
Just list all the things you haven't done
Shame's the cheapest kick to play
It makes everything OK on Judgment Day

One fine morn they'll show up at your door
Saying all they want's a little bit more
Nothing else you could've done—
You know you'll never be a chosen one

[   ]

And the grim twin fathers of gloom
Are waiting in your living room
And the gods have left everywhere
And the only game is solitaire
And all you feel is tiny and bare
But I'll watch you shoot up into air
Watch the invisible angels gather round
Watch you plummet back to ground
Cuz those gates are shut to you, baby
The joker, he figured you got that anyway

So don't heed the message on your phone
It's just a warning to try again to atone
Only now you know you're all alone
Go pour yourself another whiskey, baby
And kill your heroes before they kill you
And we'll just duck and cover down here, lover
(We'll just duck and cover)
Cuz none of this is set to end any time soon

alanaolsen

Self-Portrait

chloé lefebvre | april 2001

It doesn't seem now like that's where & when we met: during our short residencies among the snowy cragged mountains of Banff at the turn of the millennium. Alana was curled up on a couch in the café at the Centre, reading a book, a novel, sipping a latté. That novel's title—I still recall this—was *Calendar of Regrets*. In retrospect it seems perfect. Alana had scribbled all sorts of notes in the margins. Each page looked like a calculus problem. That's how she read, how she encountered the world. And while I didn't know anything about that book, I did know Alana & I were both working on films during our time up there. Her piece, *Bare*, had screened the night before. I fell in love with its menacing strangeness & wanted to meet the person who made it, thank her for dreaming it up. I asked if I could join her, treat her to another latté by way of graditude. She struck me as crazily shy. It felt like saying yes might actually cost her money. But there was also something inherently warm & welcoming & funny about her, too. She didn't hesitate smiling & gesturing to the chair beside her. We started talking, mostly just about this & that, & that's how the afternoon passed. Now it seems as if our lives had crisscrossed forever. It's been 17 years, which sounds

alanaolsen

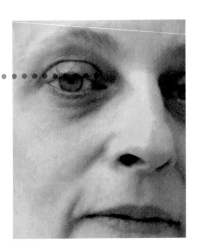

like ages, but most of our friendship took the form of dot-&-dash emails. So in one sense it lasted a long time, & in another it hardly existed at all. Now it feels as if it was over before it began. Alana sent me short, kind, beautiful notes about every film I made. I could never tell her enough how much I loved hers— especially, for me, *Self-Portrait*, the one she was working on when we met. It showed at a couple venues the year after that & then pretty much dropped off everyone's radar. But it's an amazing work. Everyone interested in experimental film should take a look. In part, I guess, it simply reminds me who Alana & I were back then, of that simple, fabulous afternoon we spent together in the café at the Banff Centre. In part it captures something deep about Alana's discomfort around other people. It's actually not a single film, but a quartet—one for each wall of the cramped room in which it's designed to appear. You enter & find your vision crammed with the large busts of many people staring at you. Some are crossing their arms. All bear nearly emotionless faces. Sound is 100% absent. The space generates a tremendous claustrophobia in the viewer. Worse, nothing changes while you stand there except almost imperceptible shifts in postures, facial muscles. You are simply being noted: perceived, briefly marked down, acknowledged, studied, assessed, judged.

Most viewers, from what I've seen, can't take it. They leave after only a couple seconds. That cramped room & those faces make you self-conscious, aware of being assembled through a mesh of power. You want to confess, apologize, cringe, argue, deny. You become the guilty kid caught with her or his hand in the cookie jar. Or an object being appraised: are you worth the price? If you do decide to linger, it slowly dawns on you the films are perpetually looping. Each is probably no longer than a minute in length, even though it feels like it could last forever. You've been placed into a position of submission ... even as you discover yourself leveling your gaze up at those leveling their gazes down at you. You become cognizant of the very act of looking, of the nature of power itself. One can't help thinking, as you stand there, of Foucault's central observation in *History of Sexuality*: that power does not refer to a general system of domination exercised by one group over another. Power doesn't work like that at all. *It seems to me*, Foucault points out instead, *that first what needs to be understood is the multiplicity of relations of force that are immanent to the domain wherein they are exercised, & that are constitutive of its organization; the game that through incessant struggle and confrontation transforms them, reinforces them, inverts them; the supports these relations of force find in each other, so as to form a chain or system*. Power,

 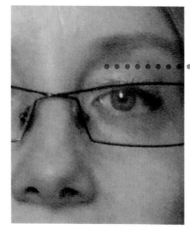

we should understand, then, is a complex, turbulent, in-process weft of energies. *Self-Portrait* asks us to contemplate that even as it makes us feel the weft instinctively. And that, I think, is why I fell in love with Alana's work in the first place. Watching it, you sense you are participating in one sort of event even as it sneaks up on you that you are actually participating in another. That's what makes her films completely hers: the ability to burst the chronic when & how we least expect it.

a city—which is unclear—sans people, filmed solely
through close-ups of its billboards at night, the impression a series of blue-ish photographs

12.

⠿ braille text ⠿

13.

2002 - 2006: olsen began 7
shorts, each of which she
abandoned

tight shot of sneakered feet walking through
abundant tall grass, no mention except on plaque
this is the massacre site of shoshone in idaho

14.

alanaolsen

one of the films was titled
a fiasco of children

15. ⠄⠇⠍⠞⠇⠓⠑⠞⠞ ⠇⠞⠕⠓⠕⠏⠞⠇⠑ ⠃⠕⠞⠓⠁
⠍⠹⠏⠽⠞⠍⠕⠦⠇⠟ ⠞⠋⠞⠹⠝⠟⠕⠑ ⠋⠄⠞⠁⠓⠕⠄
⠴⠦⠫⠟

16. 30-minutes comprised of iconic moments in film history, all mouths replaced with black rectangles, only
sound New York at rush hour

[   ]

alanaolsen

a little girl—8 or 9—reading passages from
Nietzsche's *Twilight of the Idols*, not understanding the words she mouths, but very serious

17.

another one was titled either
stay or *stray*

18.

alanaolsen

alanaolsen

Denkmal

anton jäger | sept 2006

Alana Olsen & her husband arrived in Berlin on the shortest day of 2005 for a week's vacation. On the spur of the moment, they had found a cheap set of flights from Salt Lake City to Charles de Gaulle, Charles de Gaulle to Tegel, & a cheap hotel on a sidestreet near the Tiergarten. One afternoon a fellow avant-garde filmmaker, Su Friedrich, invited them for lunch at the American Academy, an institution in Wannsee that invites 12 fellows from the U.S. (in arts, humanities, & social sciences) to live & work for an academic semester.

After they had eaten, Friedrich took the couple on a tour of the villa. They ended up on her second-floor balcony overlooking the gray drizzly lake in the leafy well-heeled suburb. On the far side, Friedrich pointed out, behind a dense stand of trees, lay the Wannsee Conference Center. On 20 January 1942 Reinhard Heydrich presided over a meeting there that lasted 85 minutes & was attended by 15 senior officials of the Nazi regime. The purpose was to set out the intellectual and ethical suicide for German culture called The Final Solution.

     The next day Olsen phoned Friedrich to ask if she might set up her camera & take several shots of the Center from Friedrich's balcony at roughly the same time each

alanaolsen

morning for the next five months, the length of Friedrich's stay at the Academy. Friedrich agreed.

Olsen's husband returned to his work as bookstore owner & manager in Salt Lake while Olsen found an inexpensive pied-à-terre in Wannsee. Olsen knocked on Friedrich's door at about 8 a.m. every day.

From 3 January through 30 May, she shot 3171 photos.

She edited those down to the 1213 she used to make *Denkmal* (the German word for *memorial*). The amalgam is 4:33 seconds long, an allusion to John Cage's pivotal non-musical work *4'33''*. Composed in 1952 for any instrument or combination of instruments, Cage's score instructs the performer(s) not to play during the three movements that comprise it.

Cage's intent, which Olsen parallels, is to show there exists no such thing as silence: every not-there contains countless there's.

The 1213 rapid-fire images of *Denkmal* create the sensation of many years rushing by. Yet we also feel barely a blink has occurred since that meeting in 1942. The Holocaust is so close to us it could be here now, unseen behind those trees.

alanaolsen

For the soundtrack Olsen created an aural collage that appropriates and repurposes several words from Adolf Eichmann's testimony during his 1961 trial in Israel. In his role as SS Lieutenant Colonel, Eichmann took minutes at the 1942 meeting. Several times during his trial he expressed satisfaction (*Zufriedenheit*) with the results of the Wannsee Conference (*zum Ergebnis der Wannsee Konferenz*). Olsen thus steals Eichmann's language even as Eichmann stole the Jews' whose extermination he oversaw, turning his words into anti-music, a soundtrack to genocide that bewilders & disturbs, urging us to move beyond reflexive accommodation.

alanaolsen

Denkmal first screened several months later (in September 2006) at the American Academy, & in rapid succession at the Institute of English and American Studies, Szeged, Hungary; the Valley Film Fest, Los Angeles, California; Situation/Event, Chicago, Illinois; & as part of three groups shows: *Time Famine* at The Antechamber, Arizona State University; *Tonguing the Zeitgeist* at Ars Bipolar, New York; & *Everything I Have Forgotten* at The Wind-Up Bird Chronicle Gallery, L.A.

The reviews were uniformly positive & primarily concentrated on Olsen's film as an examination of the ghosts that inhabit contemporary Berlin.

In a larger sense, though, *Denkmal* is also an examination of how the concept of pastness is never simply about the past. Rather, it is about the problematization of historical knowledge itself: how, to put it somewhat differently, by doing no more than moving through one's life, managing the ahistorical on an hour-to-hour basis, one is always in the process of editing, embellishing, imagining, misremembering, & fictionalizing yesterday ... as well as today and tomorrow.

The true alchemists, William Gass once commented, *do not change lead into gold; they change the world into words.*

Olsen changes world into another set of languages: optic & aural.

To wander the streets of

Berlin is to wander a gallimaufry space conducive to *dérive*. Unlike Paris or New York, it possesses no orienting axes, so every corner seems as inviting as every other to turn. Berlin is disorienting because it is disoriented. And to undertake *dérive* is to discover oneself contemplating the morality of architecture, which is to say of narrative itself: what you choose to reference, demolish, build, rebuild, augment, bury, unearth, rename.

Perhaps this impulse is what would draw Olsen's daughter to Berlin many years later: that feeling one has that Paris may always be Paris, but Berlin is never Berlin.

Everything can happen there.
Everything already has.

Small Sailboats are
Called Optimists

A Hole in the Afternoon

alanaolsen

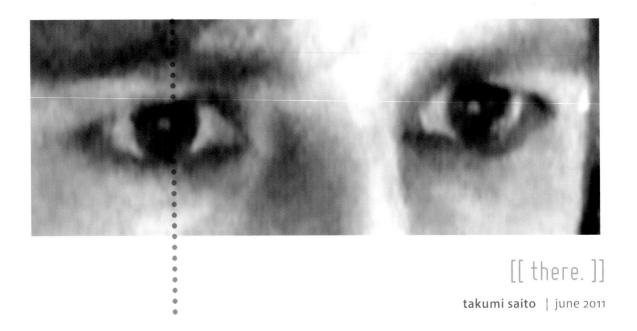

[[there.]]

takumi saito | june 2011

The relative success of Denkmal in the world of experimental film-making seems in certain ways to have perplexed & troubled Alana Olsen. For the next five years she struggled to find her way back into her work. In 2008 she tried to launch into a new film, but her efforts came to nothing. One has the impression when she couldn't bring a project to fruition she erased all vestiges of it in an attempt to clean her creative palette & prepare for her next experiment. That seems to be the case here. Unlike those artists who cannibalize abandoned work, rethinking it & folding it into future enterprises, Olsen eradicated virtually all footprints of it.

The only faint residue appears to be what Olsen's friends remember. Yet in this case Olsen seems to have been more careful than usual to keep any specific information about her in-process film from them, sharing only the fact that she was indeed working on it from early summer until late fall 2008. At that point it dropped out of her conversations. Afterward she concentrated primarily on polishing pieces for her first solo show, *Dreamlives of Debris*, which opened at The Kimball Art Center in Park City in March 2010, & on choosing several films for a group show, *The Past Unperfect*, at The Front in Manchester, New Hampshire, in August.

In September her husband & she traveled to Thailand, Cambodia, & Vietnam, a trip they had been planning for nearly a decade. While on the road Olsen began to exhibit the first signs of early-onset dementia. Upon her return her husband urged her to undergo tests to confirm their fears. Her response to the diagnosis was to return to Berlin with him in the fall & begin work on what would become her penultimate film, *[[there.]]*. The idea for it arrived during the series of musical performances the couple attended across the city. What caught Olsen's interest as she listened weren't the sonic elements, as one might expect, but rather the beautiful concentration the muscians' faces bared as they played.

In those faces, which Olsen filmed at various classical & new music concerts from October through early December, we discover muscians giving themselves over completely to presence—a *being there* that paradoxically removes the muscian from the seat, the room, the quotidian world in which he or she ostensibly resides. By being *fully there*, in other words, the player finds him or herself *somewhere else*. And hence Olsen's use of the unusual punctuation in the film's title that calls to mind Heidegger's concept of philosophical bracketing: *i.e.*, removing an object/idea from everydayness so that it can be fully thought, experienced, unconcealed.

[[there.]] *further* denaturalizes our chronic interaction with the musical moment by removing what most of us would imagine is its very essence: sound. *[[there.]]* provides us, in other words, with a soundtrack that isn't a soundtrack, with extended hush, in order to turn the visual itself into a kind of music, an interplay of shades of black & white, shapes & textures, &, once more, those rapt faces from which we can only infer the

alanaolsen

alanaolsen

music we cannot hear: both an impossible task & one we viewers catch ourselves performing unconsciously & continuously.

Such sound experiments trace a trajectory back to the very beginnings of Olsen's work as filmmaker. Although soundtrack to image in film usually bears the same relationship as text to image in narrative—manifesting a descriptive, explanatory, reinforcing function—Olsen almost from the start is attracted to the dissonance that might be exploited between acoustic & visual elements. In a sense, then, she not only brackets film itself, but also those constituent parts that make it up, including aurality.

Upon her return from Berlin, even as she began editing down the footage she had taken into what would become *[[there.]]*, she also launched into her last film, *Theories of Forgetting*, the experimental documentary about Robert Smithson's earthwork *Spiral Jetty*. Olsen chose not to attend the screenings of *[[there.]]* at *Hideous Beauties*, the group show held at The Nicholas Treadwell Gallery in Aigen, Austria, or the solo shows

alanaolsen

Head in Flames held at the 155 Project in New York or *Anxious Pleasures* at Popdom in Cologne. Rather, she decided to spend the time she had left immersing herself in Smithson's essays, making frequent visits to the *Spiral Jetty*, working on what she knew would be her final film, & simply finding moments of pleasure as best she could during her remaining years in Salt Lake City. At the end of 2011 she & her husband made a 10-day trip—her last—to Jordan to shoot footage for *Theories of Forgetting*.

Everything Already Has

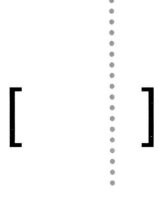

alanaolsen

Losing Things
(for A. O.)

aila olsen | april 2017

Smooth stones in rain,
your eyes are first to leave:
you can no longer find
the black smile of crow
waiting one beat before
ascending into breeze.
Your nose. Ears.
Licorice. Apple blossoms.
You misplace each
like the afternoon moon
people have forgotten
still hangs above them.

[   ]

alanaolsen

Rustle of fieldmouse
bustling through lady ferns
grays into nowhere.
Fingers, snapped twigs
cluttering your palms.
Tongue, sour taste
plumping your mouth,
is gone when you
part your hope to speak.
And so you can only dream
language now, remember,
occasionally, the orchid
early settlers found here.
It looked like a dove
& they thought it sacred
& they named it the Holy Ghost.

alanaolsen

alanaolsen

Theories of Forgetting

aila olsen | nov 2018

:::: *My mother didn't live to see* Theories of Forgetting screen at Greenhouse Berlin or Gallery 10:01 in Salt Lake City. She succumbed to complications from The Frost on 11 April 2016, more than a year & a half before those first two retrospectives of her work opened & confirmed what she had been doing almost all her life mattered to a few people.

     I wasn't there at the end. Neither was my brother. My father was, holding her hand. My mother didn't recognize him.

     Her last word was his name.

:::: *Language is punishment,* the Austrian poet Ingeborg Bachmann noticed. *All things must enter language & remain there according to the degree of their guilt.*

     My mother & I were in the car one afternoon. I don't know where we were going. I was eight or nine. Without taking her eyes off the road, almost as if she were thinking aloud to herself about something she was going to pick up at the grocery store, she

alanaolsen

announced that her biggest regret was having had children. Everything could have been so different, she said. Then she was back in this world, our world, behind the wheel, asking how my day at school had gone.

I don't miss her.

I want to make that clear.

I don't miss her & I do, more than language has the machinery to express.

We are stranded in our guilt.

Our innocence.

:::: *During her last years,* Alana Olsen became consumed by the writing & art of Robert Smithson, particularly the *Spiral Jetty*, his signature earthwork constructed over the scriptural course of six days in April 1970 on the north shore of the Great Salt Lake near an old oil rig site.

Constituted entirely of basalt, mud, salt crystals, & water, when the lake pulls back (which it does more & more these climatically catastrophic days), Smithson's achievement turns into the

Small Sailboats
Are Called

Optimists

1500-feet-long & 15-feet-wide black vertebrae of some extinct species half-buried in beige sand.

Standing before it after the two-&-a-half-hour pilgrimage from downtown along increasingly undone, poorly marked roads, you realize:

A museum can no longer be a museum, ever, a gallery no longer a gallery.

:::: *Water level & light* flux there, & so you can never visit the same earthwork twice. You discover yourself living inside the thought of an Impressionist. The momentary. The ephemeral. Wavelengths passing at 186,282 miles per second.

What an idea feels like.

:::: *Smithson & Olsen* were both drawn to the site's anti-pastoral beauty, its sense of spectacle, its disclosure of the toxic sublime, its aesthetics of waste.

That fascination, I like to imagine, is a remnant from their childhoods in rusty, slackening New Jersey.

At certain times of the year the algae in the water, which thrive in the extreme 27 percent salinity of the lake's north arm, turn a red the color of dark wine or blood.

alanaolsen

Then you are strolling along a beach at the end of everything.

:::: *You are navigating* verses from the Book of Revelations, waiting for the earthquake, the stars to rain from the sky.

If Smithson has his way (& there are those who would prefer he doesn't), *Spiral Jetty* will completely efface itself within two decades.

For nature, Smithson knew, *is never finished*.

:::: *The counterclockwise* shape is cousin to the labyrinth, archaic symbol for meditation, spiritual evolution, a journey from this plane to the next, outside to inside.

Smithson was delighted by how ubiquitous it is. The spiral occurs everywhere from megalithic art in Newgrange Tomb in County Meath, Ireland, to Op Art; from the swirl of hurricanes to nautilus shells, pine cones, & fingerprints.

The 200 billion stars that produce our Milky Way.

:::: *Entropology, the neologism* coined

alanaolsen

by Lévi-Strauss in *A World on the Wane*, palms within itself both the notions of entropy and anthropology.

    A term that doesn't exist anywhere else, but should, *entropology* should be the name *for the discipline that devotes itself to the study of* [the] *process of disintegration in its most highly evolved forms.*

:::: *Or Julian Barnes:* *What is taken away is greater than the sum of what was there. This may not be mathematically possible; but it is emotionally possible.*

:::: *The process of* disintegration, yes, but not in a negative sense, with a sense of sadness and loss.

    Rather, entropology for Smithson embodied the astonishing beauty inherent in the course of wearing down, wearing out, undoing, continuous de-creation at the level, not only of geology and thermodynamics, but also of civilizations, &, ultimately, the individuals within them.

    You. Me.

:::: *In* Theories of Forgetting, the viewer witnesses Heraclitus's cosmos unable to still itself.

    Images of Smithson's protean jetty are montaged with

That Would Be
Somebody Else's Story

[[It Always Is]]

shots of the ruins of the nearby pier & unused oil rigs, the melting façades of Petra in Jordan, rock art from southern Utah, a beating heart, Smithson's partner Nancy Holt's *Sun Tunnels*, the great open scar of the Bingham Copper Mine—0.6 miles deep, 2.5 miles wide, 1,900 acres gone, a spiral bookend at the southern tip of the lake & only man-made feature visible to the naked eye from an orbiting space shuttle.

:::: *Olsen juxtaposes* that montage with an incongruous soundtrack narrating the story of a man standing in front of a video monitor in the Istanbul Modern Art Museum.

The man has been popping various pills throughout the day (though he doesn't know what sort of drugs they contain) & his mind has loosed itself into the film he is watching ... or perhaps the film has hemorrhaged into his awareness.

The film within the film documents a performance artist dressed in a softcore maid's outfit & high heels kissing all the objects (glass coffee table, plant leaves, couch, etc.) in a strikingly white

· · · · · · · · · · · · · · · · ·

room. The observing man enters—or imagines he enters—her thoughts & experiences her obsessive joyfulness in marking her bourgeois territory like a male dog.

That woman is all of us, bought & sold by the systems that control us, by the objects they produce & we cheerfully consume, ignorant of our complicity in the matrices, incapable of envisioning our revision.

:::: *The second half* of the film involves an erasure of the first, displaying the text that makes up the observer's narrative, then letting bits of it fade away (a linguistic sort of entropy) to reveal a second story implicit in the first. This one is recited by a woman (my mother) & cancels out (or at least agitates) the male's voice that narrates the film's first half.

:::: *Which is to say:* What is taken away is greater than the sum of what was there in the first place.

Quantity always functions as an irrational number.

My mother will always be inconceivable.

She leaves us with more than we can imagine, more than we could ever want, more than we will ever be able to leave behind.

alanaolsen

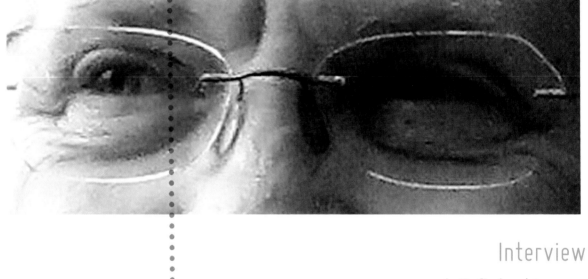

Interview

katja fischer | june 2011

I am sitting in front of my computer in Aigen, Austria. It is a week before Alana Olsen's film *[[there.]]* screens at *Hideous Beauties*, the group show opening here on the solstice at The Nicholas Treadwell Gallery. Olsen is sitting in front of her computer in Salt Lake City in the U.S. state of Utah. We are Skyping. She has asked me not to use video or audio & so we are messaging instead.

Fischer: You've decided not to attend the opening later this week at which *[[there.]]* will be screened. Would you care to talk a little about your decision?

Olsen: I don't like crowds. I don't like travel. I don't like meeting new people. Planes & questions frighten me.

Fischer: But *[[there.]]* is an extraordinarily powerful work. I'm sure many would love to hear how & what the filmmaker herself thinks about it.

Olsen: Honestly, I don't have all that much important to say about it or any other film I've made.

Fischer: That might surprise some viewers of your work.

Olsen: Artists already talk too much about what they do. I don't want to add to the noise. The more you listen, the less you understand what they're talking about.

Fischer: Have you missed other openings where your work was shown?

Olsen: Lots. The U.S. cares less & less about things like art, literature, & serious music, & more & more about intense modes of forgetting called entertainment.

Fischer: That's why you don't go?

Olsen: Not many places screen my work to begin with. Many writers feel compelled to give readings, many musicians to perform their work. I feel compelled to stay home.

Fischer: At the risk of trespassing into territory you may not wish to enter, could you talk a moment about *[[there.]]*—where the idea came from, how it grew into its present form, what interests you most about it?

Olsen: I genuinely don't remember where the idea came from anymore, or even how, exactly, it grew into itself. I tend to draw a blank about that kind of thing as soon as I'm finished with something. My unconscious seems to believe it's time to move on & hits the delete key.

Fischer: And the dimensions of the film that interest you?

alanaolsen

Olsen: I wouldn't want to pin anything down in particular.

Fischer: You're known for your sound experiments. They form an integral dialogue with & frequently counterpoint to what's happening visually in your works.

Olsen: I take some solace in not being known for much of anything. I just like to make films I want to watch. I do that because it pleases me. They don't usually end up saying what I want them to say, but that's my problem. It's beyond me how some artists get what's going on in their heads up onto a screen.

Fischer: Do you think that might be because a film you've made is still part of your ongoing personal experience? Perhaps it's difficult for any piece of art to catch up to the artist.

Olsen: How could you ever figure out such things? Anyway, I don't do well explaining stuff. I always end up saying something I don't mean in my interviews & films. Afterward I feel like an idiot & have to start all over again. I'm guessing that's the crux of being an artist.

alanaolsen

Fischer: You don't like photos or videos of yourself taken.

Olsen: I've already inadvertently been in more than enough vacation photos & videos.

Fischer: I was wondering about your instinct to capture instants that are difficult for most of us to see—how people lower their heads to erase feigned happiness in *Where the Smiling Ends*, the spellbound look in the musicians' faces in *[[there.]]*.

Olsen: A lot of people don't experience what they experience. They think they do, but instead they experience what they expect to experience, which is to say what they've been taught to experience. They experience those smiles, the muscians' music. But I'm not interested in looking at the perfectly composed shot. I'm interested in looking at the one that happens just after that. Or maybe just outside the frame of it. We become different people—if, admittedly, only in tiny ways—watching such filmic moments.

Fischer: Which filmmakers have had the most lasting influence on your work?

Olsen: The answer seems to change every day.

Fischer: What does it feel like when you're deep into a project—into the presentness of creation?

Olsen: It feels like architecture. It feels like walking through a complex building you've never walked through before. Every hall, room, is a brief amazement.

Fischer: How, if at all, do you sense being a woman filmmaker inflects your engagement with your medium?

Olsen: I'm not sure I could address that without rehearsing a laundry list of hackneyed assumptions about what it means to be a woman or a man. Do people still really answer questions like that? It seems fraught with credulity.

Fischer: Which of your films have stayed with you most over the years?

Olsen: None. I've forgotten them all equally. Or maybe they've all forgotten me.

alanaolsen

Fischer: Would you say, then, that your work in certain ways is ultimately about the act of unknowing?

Olsen: I would say my work is ultimately about the act of un-learning. I like being baffled.

Fischer: How has living in Salt Lake City for so long helped form you as a filmmaker?

Olsen: The light's completely different here from anywhere else. And the shockingly stark mountains on every horizon. There's the backbeat of that preposterous religion, of course. Otherwise, not a lot. Still, when I go elsewhere I do feel different, if not in a paraphraseable way, & when I return to Salt Lake I feel a sense of relief, maybe just because it's nice to be inconspicuous. I value the camouflaged.

Fischer: And being a mother?

Olsen: It's nice to be inconspicuous.

Fischer: In what sense?

Olsen: All of them.

Fischer: Have you ever thought about working in another medium—writing, for example, or hypermedia?

Olsen: Your question is like asking a bricklayer if he ever contemplated becoming an audiologist or actuary. It's beyond my imaginative capabilities.

Fischer: What are you working on now?

Olsen: Nothing special.

Fischer: What advice would you give a younger version of yourself at the outset of your career as an innovative filmmaker?

Olsen: I'd say: *You'll work till you're blind & probably get nothing for it. You'll crave recognition & probably get none. If you're original, really original, you'll make virtually no money from your art & have no impact on anyone & will have to make a living some other way, which will probably disappoint you.*

Fischer: That sounds grim.

Olsen: If so, chances are you're not an artist. I'd also add: *Everyone thinking about becoming a filmmaker should take a course on how not to become a filmmaker.*

Fischer: Because most courses simply teach you how to follow formulae?

Olsen: Because if you take a course on how not to become a filmmaker you have an outside chance of living semi-happily ever after.

Fischer: Thank you for answering my questions.

Olsen: I'd tell that younger version of myself, *if you don't feel like making films anymore, consider yourself lucky. You're cured.*

Fischer: Is there anything else you'd like to add?

Olsen: No. I've probably said too much already.

[   ]

alanaolsen

alanaolsen

acknowledgements

The author wishes to thank the following for helping dream the Olsens: Kathrin Anhold, Kerstin Apel, David Barclay, Ralph Berry, Emma & Noam Braslavsky, Andreas Bräutigam, Mark Carlson, Chloe Rachel, Gene Coleman, Lucy Corin, Beth Couture, DAAD Artists-in-Berlin Program, Samuel R. Delany, Martin Dimitrov, John-Thomas Eltringham, Su Friedrich, Ensemble PHACE, Ensemble Resonanz, Ensemble unitedberlin, Lutz Finkl, Greenhouse Berlin, Gayle Gutierrez, Christian Hawkey, Ellen Hinsey, Shelley Jackson, Japanese-German Center Berlin, Emma Karlsson, Reinold Kegel, Anika Kettelhake, Michael Kroetch, Michael Leong, MaerzMusik Festival 2013 Berliner Festspiele, R. Jay Magill, Larry McCaffery, Christina Milletti, Tine Mitzlaff, Lance Olsen, Andi Olsen, Rochelle Ratner, Wayne & Marlette Rebhorn, Carol Scherer, Davis Schneiderman, Oliver Schneller, The American Academy in Berlin, Uljana Wolf, Lidia Yuknavitch

alanaolsen

alanaolsen

in collaboration with aila olsen

alanaolsen

&NOW Books

Carnegie Hall

Lake Forest College

555 N. Sheridan Road

Lake Forest, IL 60045

ISBN: 978-1-941423-93-6

andnow@lakeforest.edu

lakeforest.edu/andnow